W9-ANO-012

Spring Is Here!
A Story About Seeds

By Joan Holub
Illustrated by Will Terry

Ready-to-Read • Aladdin
New York London Toronto Sydney

For Sheri Leider,
with thanks –J. H.

For Jocelyn –W. T.

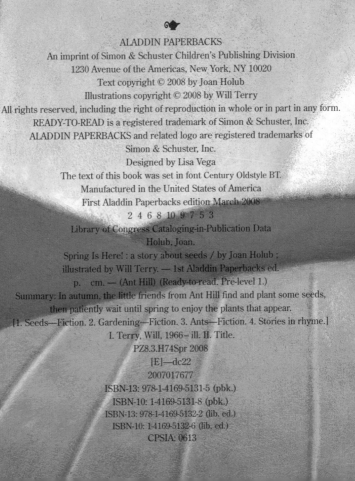

ALADDIN PAPERBACKS
An imprint of Simon & Schuster Children's Publishing Division
1230 Avenue of the Americas, New York, NY 10020
Text copyright © 2008 by Joan Holub
Illustrations copyright © 2008 by Will Terry
Designed by Lisa Vega
The text of this book was set in font Century Oldstyle BT.
Manufactured in the United States of America
First Aladdin Paperbacks edition March 2008
2 4 6 8 10 9 7 5 3
Library of Congress Cataloging-in-Publication Data
Holub, Joan.
Spring Is Here! : a story about seeds / by Joan Holub ;
illustrated by Will Terry. — 1st Aladdin Paperbacks ed.
p.   cm. — (Ant Hill) (Ready-to-read. Pre-level 1.)
Summary: In autumn, the little friends from Ant Hill find and plant some seeds,
then patiently wait until spring to enjoy the plants that appear.
[1. Seeds—Fiction. 2. Gardening—Fiction. 3. Ants—Fiction. 4. Stories in rhyme.]
I. Terry, Will, 1966– ill. II. Title.
PZ8.3.H74Spr 2008
[E]—dc22
2007017677
ISBN-13: 978-1-4169-5131-5 (pbk.)
ISBN-10: 1-4169-5131-8 (pbk.)
ISBN-13: 978-1-4169-5132-2 (lib. ed.)
ISBN-10: 1-4169-5132-6 (lib. ed.)
CPSIA: 0613

"A seed," says Reed.

"Lots more!"
says Tor.

"Plant them,"
says Em.

"Add dirt,"
says Curt.

"Now grow!" says Joe.

"Just wait," says Kate.

"A drip,"
says Chip.

"Lots more!"
says Tor.

"Yay! Rain!"
says Jane.

"Splish, splash,"
goes Nash.

"Splash, splish,"
goes Trish.

"A lake!" says Jake.

"Dive in,"
says Lynn.

"A raft," says Taft.

"Hop on,"
says Dawn.

"Blue sky,"
says Guy.

"Rainbow!" yells Joe.

"Hey, look," says Brook.

"A stem," says Jem.

"And leaves,"
says Reeves.

"A bud," says Judd.

"Blooms, too,"
says Drew.

"Lots more!"
says Tor.

"Spring is here!"

The ants cheer.